# WEDDING

# FLOWERS

THE • COBBLE • STREET • COUSINS

# WEDDING
# FLOWERS

# CYNTHIA RYLANT

*illustrated by*

# WENDY ANDERSON HALPERIN

SCHOLASTIC INC.
New York  Toronto  London  Auckland  Sydney
Mexico City  New Delhi  Hong Kong  Buenos Aires

ISBN 0-439-87720-2

Text copyright © 2002 by Cynthia Rylant.
Illustrations copyright © 2002 by Wendy Anderson Halperin.
All rights reserved. Published by Scholastic Inc.,
557 Broadway, New York, NY 10012,
by arrangement with
Simon & Schuster Books for Young Readers,
Simon & Schuster Children's Publishing Division.
SCHOLASTIC and associated logos are trademarks
and/or registered trademarks of Scholastic Inc.

12 11 10 9 8 7 6 5 4 3 2 1          6 7 8 9 10 11/0

Printed in the U.S.A.          40

First Scholastic printing, April 2006

Book design by Mark Siegel
The text of this book is set in Garth Graphic.
The illustrations are rendered in pencil and watercolor.

# TABLE OF
# CONTENTS

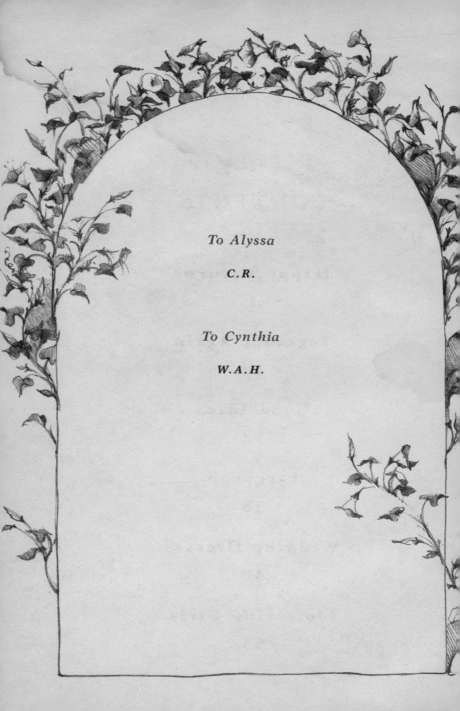

*To Alyssa*

*C.R.*

*To Cynthia*

*W.A.H.*

# WEDDING

# FLOWERS

## HAPPY RETURNS

𝒥t was August and on Cobble Street the pretty blue house with red geraniums by the door had been quiet for much of the summer. No nighttime giggles and whispers could be heard in the attic. The kitchen was always very clean (there was hardly any cookie baking going on). And the front porch surely needed a cat.

All of this, however, was about to change—
for the Cobble Street cousins were
coming back!

Lily, Rosie, and Tess—three girls
all now ten years old—had lived in

this sweet blue house with their aunt Lucy for nearly a year. In fact, they had lived here for all of fourth grade while their parents traveled with the ballet.

Each had slept in her own little bed in the attic, where Lily had written her poems, her sister Rosie had played with her dolls, and their cousin Tess had practiced singing songs.

Tess's cat, Elliott, had also lived with them. And he had slept where he wanted to. Elliott had loved Aunt Lucy's house as much as the girls did.

4

But when the
summer came, the
girls' parents had
returned and the
cousins had left Aunt
Lucy's house. Lily
and Rosie had gone

back to their own house, many
miles away, and Tess and Elliott
had gone to theirs, even
more miles
away.
But
the
cousins
wrote
so many letters
and notes back and forth, it hardly seemed
they were separated at all:

Dear Tess and Elliot,
Today Rosie bought red bubble bath and now the bathtub is all pink! So are Rosie's toes!
Love Lily and Rosie (who's very rosie)

Dear Lily and Rosie
We are sending a L.O.N.G letter because we long to see you!
So long,
Love, Tess and Elliot

Dear Elliot,
Here is some catnip for you and you don't have to share it with Tess.
Love, Lily and Tess

★ DEAR
LILY and Rosie
Today I hit a high note and now I sound all SWEAKY I think my birthday career is ruined.
Love, Tess
P.S. But I still can dance

Dear Tess,
Here is a lollypop for you and you do not have to share it with Elliot. Love, Lily and Rosie

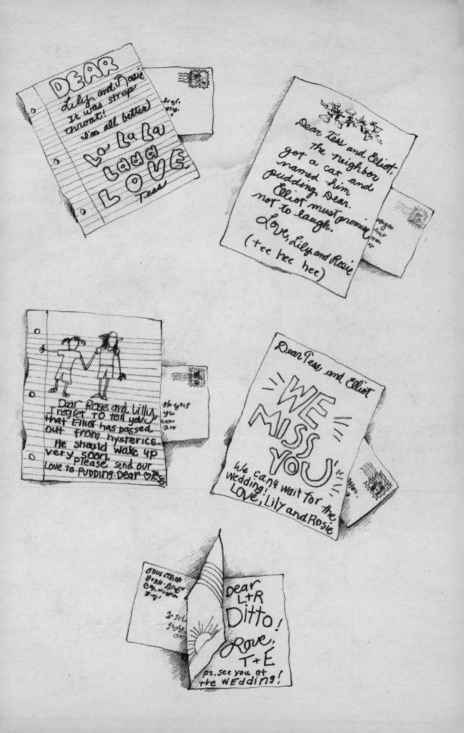

The *wedding* the cousins were so thrilled about and so looking forward to was that of their Aunt Lucy and her sweetheart, Michael. The cousins had introduced Michael to Aunt Lucy, so they felt very proud and happy about the way things had worked out.

*Plus* Aunt Lucy had actually asked them to help with the wedding! She said they were best at making things fun. And as if that weren't exciting enough, Aunt Lucy wanted all three girls to be her bridesmaids!

So now the cousins were on their way back to Cobble Street

9

—two by train and one by plane (with a certain cat nicely tucked under her seat)—and everyone was as happy as could be. A wedding was in store!

Michael met Lily and Rosie at the train station. When the girls walked into the terminal and saw him standing there, they dropped all their bags and boxes and books and nearly

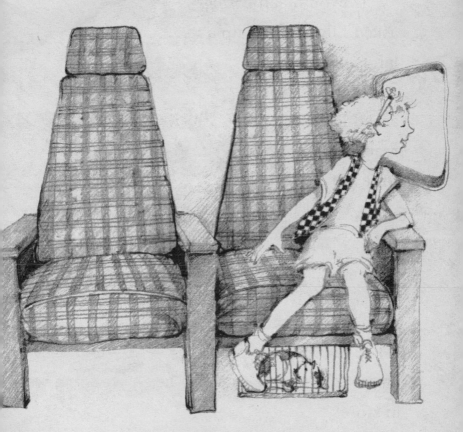

knocked him down with their happy hugs.

"Cousins!" said Michael, grinning shyly.
"It's great to see you. Life is so different without you."

"Do you mean *boring?*"
asked Lily, picking up a
large bag.

"And *dull?*"
asked Rosie,
reaching
for a box.

"Exactly," said Michael, filling his arms
with the rest of the girls' things.

*"Good!"* said Lily and
Rosie, smiling
happily.

"Ready to go to
Cobble Street?" asked
Michael. "Tess and
Elliott should
be there by
now."

Rosie
sighed.

"Cobble Street," she said
with satisfaction.

"Music to my ears," said
Lily.

On the way to Aunt
Lucy's house, the two girls

told Michael what they'd been doing in the summer weeks since they'd last seen him.

"Lily joined a writing club at the library," said Rosie.

"And Rosie's taking a pottery class," said Lily.

"I'm not very good at it," said Rosie. "My pots go *bloop-bloop-bloop* off the wheel."

Michael smiled.

"What have *you* been doing, Michael?" asked Lily. "Are you taking summer classes?" (Michael was studying to be a botanist.)

15

"Actually, I've been helping Lucy with the house," he said. "I fixed the leaky roof, painted the parlor, replaced three steps, and regrouted the sink."

"Wow," said Rosie.

"I also mashed my thumb, sprained my ankle, bruised my head, and fell off a ladder," Michael added.

Rosie giggled and giggled.

"That's just what *I* would do," she said.

"I know," said Michael with a big grin. "We're alike in that way."

Rosie felt so happy. Michael remembered they were a lot alike. He was going to be a wonderful uncle.

As if Lily were reading Rosie's mind, she asked, "Should we call you 'Uncle Michael'?"

"You can call me whatever you like," said Michael. He thought a moment. "Homer. You can call me Homer if you like. Or maybe Otis."

Lily laughed.

"I like Otis," she said.

"How about Goober?" asked Rosie.

"Or Dumpling," added Lily.

"Sparky?"

"Rover?"

All the way to Cobble Street everyone was laughing over some very silly names.

## TOGETHER AGAIN

"**T**ESS!" cried Lily and Rosie.

There was their dear sweet cousin, skipping down the front steps to meet them.

Tess threw her arms around the two girls.

"Together again AT LAST!" she said dramatically. (Tess was usually dramatic.)

"I like your sneakers, Tess," said Rosie.

"I like *your* shirt," said Tess. "And Lily's necklace."

"I like your hat," said Lily.

"I LOVE you both!" cried Tess, hugging them again. "I've missed you so much."

Michael finished unloading the car, then joined them with his arms full of bags and boxes and books.

"Hi, Tess," he said with a big smile.

"Hey!" said Tess. "Aren't you that guy who's going to be my UNCLE?"

She gave Michael a hug around all the luggage.

"If I survive the unloading," he answered with a grin.

"Wait'll you see how much stuff *I* brought,"

said Tess. "Aunt Lucy and I had to make eight trips back and forth from the taxi.

"Plus," she added, "I brought the best thing of all. . . ."

22

*"Elliott!"* cried Lily and Rosie.

They ran up the steps.

In the kitchen Aunt Lucy was just pouring Elliott a little bowl of cream.

"Cousins!" she said, her arms opening wide.

There were more hugs and more "I-missed-you's" while patient

Elliott was cuddled by one cousin, then another, then another before he could lap up his cream.

The girls gathered around the big kitchen table while Aunt Lucy and Michael brought out a lovely bowl of strawberries and a plate of macaroons and a nice cold pitcher of pink lemonade.

"Aunt Lucy," said Tess, "there is no better kitchen in the world than yours."

"No better house," added Lily.

"Or napkins," said Rosie.

*"Napkins?"* asked Tess.

"See?" said Rosie. "Little petunias," she said, holding up her napkin.

Aunt Lucy smiled and stroked Rosie's hair.

"You always love the small things, Rosie," she said.

"Speaking of small things," said Michael, reaching into his pocket.

He brought forth three tiny wrapped boxes and set them on the table.

"They're from Lucy and me," he said.

"Oh my goodness!" said Lily.

"Cool!" said Tess.

"Wow," said Rosie.

Aunt Lucy smiled.

"You may open them now, if you like," she said.

With wide eyes, each of the cousins picked up her own small gift.

"First let's unwrap them," said Tess. "Then let's open them at the same time."

"Okay," answered Lily and Rosie.

The girls carefully removed the paper and ribbons.

"Okay?" asked Tess.

Lily and Rosie nodded.

"Open!" said Tess.

Each girl removed the lid from her small box. And all three girls gasped with delight at what they saw.

For inside each box was a delicate silver bracelet, bearing a single silver charm.

"Mine has a cottage charm!" exclaimed Rosie, lifting hers up.

"I have a record player!" said Tess.

"And I have a typewriter charm!" said Lily.

"*Thank you!*" all three girls cried, hugging Aunt Lucy and Michael all over again.

"The bracelets are to say thank you—from Michael and me—for bringing us together," Aunt Lucy said.

Michael nodded in agreement.

"And we thought," continued

Aunt Lucy, "that each summer when you come to stay with us, we'll add a new charm."

"They'll be 'good future' charms," said Michael. "Whatever is new and good in your life, we'll add a charm to celebrate it."

"Wow," said Tess. "I hope I get a star charm, for being the star of a musical."

"I hope I get an Eiffel Tower charm," Lily said with a smile, "when I go to Paris."

"I'd like a puppy," said Rosie.

Aunt Lucy helped each cousin put on her bracelet.

"Whatever the charms may be," she said, "they'll celebrate really wonderful things in your lives. And we can't even begin to guess what those will be."

"Like you," said Rosie. "You didn't guess you'd find Michael."

"Right," said Aunt Lucy.

"He's *your* charm," said Tess.

"Your Prince *Charm*-ing," added Lily.

"Not in these socks," said Michael. "I just noticed them."

Everyone looked down at Michael's feet.

One sock was blue, the other green.

"I do that all the time," said Rosie. "Except I have cows."

Everyone looked at Rosie for a silent moment, then they all burst into laughter.

It was so good to be together again, there in Aunt Lucy's kitchen.

## GOOD IDEAS

*A*unt Lucy and Michael had decided they wanted a Saturday morning wedding because morning was their favorite time of day. They wanted a small wedding, in Aunt Lucy's backyard, where blue morning glories twined around the arbor and hollyhocks climbed the picket fence.

And they had asked the cousins if the girls
might plan the after-wedding breakfast treats
for everyone. The cousins—especially Rosie—
were delighted!

They huddled together in the cozy attic that
first night back—in their old Playground in the
middle of the room—and excitedly began
making plans.

"I have an idea," said Rosie, holding her bright yellow notepad (each cousin had a notepad). "Since Aunt Lucy owns a flower shop, let's make breakfast look like flowers."

"Good idea!" said Lily.

"How about Sunflower Cinnamon Biscuits?" asked Rosie.

"Rosie, you are a *genius*," said Tess. "We'll find a big sunflower cookie cutter."

"We can even use tiny cookie cutters to make the butter in pretty shapes," said Lily.

"And Michael loves strawberry jam," said Rosie. "I know, because I do too and we

talked about it once."

"You talk about the

strangest things, Rosie," said Tess.

Rosie grinned.

"Anyway," she said, "we can serve the jam in little cups decorated with real flower petals. We can glue them on."

"We should serve cheese, too," said Lily.

"If we use soft cheese," said Tess, "we can form it into any shape we want."

"How about leaves?" asked Rosie. "Since Michael studies botany? We could make cheese leaves and put them on a big platter."

"And sprinkle green stuff—maybe parsley—on top so they'll look real," said Lily.

"We need fruit," said Tess.

"Grapes are good," said Rosie. "They won't get all mushy."

"Cherries too," added Lily.

"We could use those sticks they make shish kebab with," said Tess. "And slide the grapes and cherries on."

"With real flowers," said Rosie, "that people can actually eat. Like pansies."

*"Perfect!"* cried Lily. "Is anyone writing this down?"

"Oops," said Rosie and Tess.

"How do you spell 'shish kebab'?" asked Rosie, lifting her pen.

Everyone grinned. This was so much fun!

FERGUSON

The next day Aunt Lucy invited the cousins to meet the priest who would perform the wedding.

"I have to stop by his office," said Aunt Lucy. "Would you girls like to come along? His name is Father Frank and he and Michael grew up together. He also has a little dog named Ferguson who always wears a red plaid jacket."

38

"Great!" said the cousins. "Let's go!"

"Has Ferguson met Yardley?" Rosie asked on the way to the church. Yardley was a basset hound who belonged to Michael's father. Michael often took care of Yardley, and the cousins all loved the hound. He was slow, pudgy, and thoroughly sweet.

"The dogs haven't met yet," said Aunt Lucy. "But they're both invited to the wedding, so they'll meet soon."

"I hope Ferguson likes cats," said Tess, thinking of Elliott.

40

"I think Ferguson likes everything and everyone," said Aunt Lucy. "But he loves his jacket most of all. He won't leave the house without it."

The three cousins giggled.

At the rectory Aunt Lucy introduced the girls to Father Frank, a young man who was sporting a beard and rather long hair.

"You look sort of cool for a priest," said Tess, shaking his hand.

*"Tess!"* said Lily, eyes wide. Tess always said what she thought and Lily always said *"Tess!"* when she did. Rosie just grinned.

Father Frank grinned, too.

"I wish you'd tell that to the Bishop," he said. "He always says my hair is too long."

"Sure, I'll call him!" said Tess.

Father Frank laughed.

"I'll bet you would," he answered. "Luckily, the Bishop loves Ferguson, so he's pretty nice to me, too."

"Where *is* Ferguson?" asked Rosie.

"He's in the courtyard," said Father Frank. "Would you like to meet him?"

"We can't wait!" said Lily.

The cousins followed Father Frank to the interior courtyard of the church. And there they saw little Ferguson, wearing his red plaid jacket, sleeping at the foot of a large, beautiful angel.

"He looks . . . *heavenly*," whispered Lily.

"I think God really likes Ferguson," whispered Rosie.

"Me too," said Father Frank with a smile. He gave a short whistle.

"Ferguson!" he called.

Up jumped the little dog in a snap. He bounded

over to Father Frank and his visitors and soon the cousins were all on the grass with the funny dog, rolling and laughing and getting many good dog kisses.

"Father Frank and I will be inside his office for a few minutes," Aunt Lucy told the girls. "Do you mind waiting here?"

"Stay all day!" said Tess, giggling as Ferguson ran circles around her. "We're in heaven!"

Aunt Lucy grinned.

"I believe you are," she said.

And as Aunt Lucy returned inside the church, the cousins played with Ferguson beneath the wings of an angel.

# WEDDING DRESSES

On Wednesday the cousins were to see what they would be wearing at the wedding. Aunt Lucy had asked them to wait, telling them that their dresses weren't quite ready. But on Wednesday it was time.

"We'll go over to Mrs. White's house after tea," Aunt Lucy told the girls.

"The dresses are there?" asked Tess.

"Actually, yes." Aunt Lucy smiled. "Believe it or not, I sewed them myself. Mrs. White taught me how."

"Wow!" said all three girls.

"Mrs. White is the best," said Rosie.

"I agree." Aunt Lucy nodded her head.

"Let's get through tea in a hurry!" said Tess.

After a cup of tea and a blueberry muffin (they also wrapped some muffins for Mrs. White), the cousins were off. As they approached Mrs. White's small house, Aunt

Lucy said, "I do hope you like the dresses. I'm a little nervous about it."

"Don't worry, Aunt Lucy," said Lily. "We love *everything* you do."

Aunt Lucy smiled gratefully.

Mrs. White met everyone at the door.

"Dear girls!" she said, giving each a kiss on the cheek. "How we've all missed you!"

"We've missed you, too," said Rosie.

"Come in, come in." Mrs. White led them into her cozy, old-fashioned living room. On the sofa were three soft

parcels wrapped in tissue, each bearing a
cousin's name.

"Ooh," said Lily, seeing them. "I can't
wait."

Mrs. White and
Aunt Lucy sat down

to watch the cousins unwrap their dresses.

The girls picked up their packages.

"Ready?" said Tess. "Open!"

Within seconds the tissue was off and the cousins were holding up their three beautiful dresses, all in *flowers*.

"I have lilies!" said Lily.

"Mine are tulips!" said
Tess. "I *love* tulips!"

"Of course mine are
roses," said Rosie, giggling.

"I hope you like them," said
Aunt Lucy.

"We *adore* them!" cried
Lily.

The cousins all gave
Aunt Lucy giant hugs before
running to try on their dresses.

When they returned
wearing them, Mrs.
White applauded.

"I've never seen
more lovely brides-
maids," she said.

"We'll put flowers in

your hair," said Aunt Lucy. "And, of course, in your hands."

"Weddings are so . . . so . . .," said Lily.

*"Flowery,"* finished Tess.

"Yes!" said Rosie. "Isn't it fun?"

The cousins were so happy.

FLOWERING GIRLS

$\mathcal{D}$aybreak on Saturday was beautiful. The rising sun made the dew glisten on the backyard morning glories. The birds sang their morning songs. And the world was calm and lovely.

The cousins knew this because the cousins were all *wide awake* in their attic! As was Aunt Lucy, already in her bath. And Michael, nervously pruning the plants in his apartment. Everyone was *excited*. And awake.

The cousins hurried downstairs to Aunt Lucy's kitchen to prepare the wedding breakfast. The Sunflower Cinnamon Biscuits had been mixed and cut the night before, and only had to be baked. Skewers were ready for the

grapes, cherries, and pansies. Little cups of jam had been decorated with rose petals. And all of the cheese leaves had been designed and needed only a sprinkle of parsley.

The cousins had also decided on a big glass

bowl full of orange juice punch. And Mrs. White would be bringing tiny apple fritters. (*"Yum,"* said Rosie, who planned to get the recipe.)

The cousins worked quickly inside the house, preparing the small tables (Aunt Lucy had found wonderful flowered cloths to cover them).

Soon the cousins were bounding back up

the stairs to clean up and put on their beautiful dresses. Then bounding back downstairs to find Aunt Lucy and receive their flowers.

They found Aunt Lucy in the parlor, quietly sorting everyone's bouquets, humming, and looking more beautiful than they'd ever seen her. She wore a simple white embroidered dress with tiny pearl buttons on the collar and lace at the edges of the sleeves. Her hair was as she'd always worn it, except now it was decorated with a headband of small white roses and satin rosettes. Her shoes were old-fashioned buckle-ons, shiny white.

"Aunt Lucy," said Tess, "we are speechless." The other two cousins nodded.

Aunt Lucy blushed.

"It's fun to be a bride," she said with a shy smile.

"And look at *you*, you beautiful, wonderful,

flowering girls!" she added. "Let's decorate your hair!"

When the cousins were all decorated with lovely sprigs and petals, Aunt Lucy stepped back to admire them.

"I think I'm going to cry," she said.

"Don't cry," said Tess. "You'll get all soppy."

Aunt Lucy grinned.

"Well, I wouldn't want to get all soppy," she said. "Let's find Elliott and wait for our guests."

Soon everyone began arriving. The girls' parents from the hotel in town. Mr. French, with a big basket of peaches from his market. Mrs. White, with apple fritters, and her friend Senator Harrison. Michael's sister from Chicago. Michael's

father (who
the cousins
hadn't yet
met) and his
dog, Yardley
(who wanted to lick

the flowers from their hair).

Finally, Michael and Father
Frank and Ferguson all arrived
together. Ferguson wore a
white carnation pinned to his
red plaid jacket. And Michael
looked, for the first time,
unrumpled. He also had a
cactus tie.

"Cool tie," said Tess.

"Thank you," said Michael,
bowing in friendly formality.
"And where is the bride?"

Just as he asked, Aunt Lucy—who had shown her guests inside—stepped out onto the porch.

Looking at Aunt Lucy and Michael's face when he saw her, the cousins nearly *did* cry. For it was real love they saw in that moment. And each girl would always remember it.

The backyard wedding was quiet, lovely, and simple. The dogs were perfect. Elliott slept on top of the arbor. And before the cousins knew it, Aunt

Lucy and Michael had said, "I do."

Afterward, as everyone filled their plates with breakfast treats, the girls gave the bride and groom a special wrapped present.

"We made it for you," said Lily. "I wrote the poem on the first page."

Michael and Aunt Lucy sat down on the backyard swing and opened their gift.

It was a handmade scrapbook, titled *Our Life*. Underneath the title was a photo of Michael and Aunt Lucy, taken on Aunt Lucy's front porch.

They turned to page one. And it read:

*Grow flowers in your garden*
*Grow apples in your trees*
*Grow kitties in your kitchen*
*Grow lots of minty teas.*
*Grow baskets full of babies*
*Grow days of happiness*
*Grow old and dear together*
*And don't forget to kiss.*
*We love you,*
*The Cobble Street Cousins*

Aunt Lucy's eyes filled with tears.

"It's okay," said Tess. "You can get soppy now."

Michael squeezed Aunt Lucy's hand and turned the page. At the top of the next page the cousins had printed the words "Our Favorite Tree."

"You have to put a photograph on that page," said Rosie.

Tess nudged her.

"They know that," Tess said.

"Well, maybe they thought they had to draw it," said Rosie. "I would."

"I did," said Michael.

"See?" Rosie giggled.

Page after page, the cousins had chosen things for Aunt Lucy and Michael to remember:

"Our Front Door"

"Our Garden"

"Our Favorite Poem"

"Our Favorite Birds"

"Our Best Thoughts"

"Our Best Cats"

"Our Couch"

"I picked the couch," said Tess, grinning.

Finally, on the last page, Aunt Lucy and Michael read, "Our Babies."

Lily smiled.

"We could use the money," she said. "We'll be old enough to baby-sit in a couple of years."

Aunt Lucy stood up and drew the cousins close to her.

"In the meantime," she said, "*you* can be our babies."

"Good," said Rosie. "I'm not ready to grow up yet."

"Neither am I," said Lily.

"I am," said Tess, "but I'll wait for you guys."

"Thank you for this, girls," said Michael. "Thank you for *everything*."

"When you get back from your honeymoon at the lighthouse, will you send us pictures?" asked Rosie.

"Definitely," said Michael.

"And will you leave our attic just the way it is, until next summer?" asked Lily.

"We won't touch a thing," said Michael.

Aunt Lucy lifted Rosie's small arm and

touched the silver bracelet on her wrist.

"Good futures," she said, smiling.

And each cousin knew in her heart, standing there in the garden of that beloved blue house, that what Aunt Lucy said was true.

Good futures were waiting.

"Let's go find the dogs!" said Rosie.

"Let's go!" said Lily and Tess.

The cousins took hands and, flowers flying, ran across the yard to play.

72